DENISE LESLEY

The Cabin Child

Copyright 2021 By Denise Lesley

First published in 2021 by Kindle Direct Publishing

Other works by Denise Lesley

The Curse of the Princess (first published in 2021 by KDP)

ACKNOWLEDGEMENT

Thank you to my family and Ben for always supporting me and helping me with ideas.
Love always.

Eight months ago, Amelia did not think she was about to embark on a journey to motherhood. No woman in the world has been pregnant for seven years, not since the runners arrived, not since women around the world would get to a certain point in their pregnancy and suffer internal bleeding and not survive.

Doctors did not know what came first the virus in the adults, or the virus in the foetus', what they did know was how bad everything was going to get. The nurses whispering in the corridors, rummers that the doctors were stabbing people in the heads once the machines determine the patients are dead, or no brain activity.

The media caught wind of it somehow but doctors and politicians alike kept it secret and reassured everyone that everything was normal.

Amelia and her husband Jason knew that their baby would change the world, to save it, but they had far bigger problems than they ever thought they would have. Not because of the runners, they are just there and inconvenient now, but with the human race.

Everything started to go wrong when a virus hit the globe, it would trigger something in the brain of those infected to kill and eat other humans, as soon as they were bitten the virus would take over and they would move on to the next available healthy person. Things turned nasty quickly, first it was the police that attempted to stop it, then the government told the army to get involved, very soon after that people were being evacuated from the cities, or were to be bombed with the runners, more and more people were being infected, dying and moving on to their next victim. It took about 2 months for the worlds population to drop, and for those who escaped to just survive.

Seven years on and far less people were coming to the camp sites looking for refuge around England. Most of the communication had stopped with the sites North of England and the South was just as quiet. Now it was just one camp for itself, they learned to farm, generate clean water and be safe by putting up large fences using what they could to keep the runners out if any came wondering into the countryside.

◆ ◆ ◆

Let's start from the beginning. With Amelia and Jason. Two very ordinary people, with ordinary jobs. Amelia was in the office the day the outbreak was shown to the world. The T.V was on showing round the world news when the news reporter was interrupted;

'We have some breaking news for you, an attack in London causing panic in the underground, we're going live to John Term. John can you tell us anything about these attacks?'

The camera flickers and John is standing at the entrance to the Waterloo underground, his brown hair fluttering in the wind, his shirt undone at the top. Temperatures had been soaring over the months and London was at 35 degrees. John's shirt was dark with sweat, he had clearly been running to get to the location to capture the story. He was slightly out of breath and the light from the camera clearly showed the beads forming on his forehead.

'Yes, Judy I can. It is believed a man from unknown origin is currently being pursued by police for attacking members of the public by biting them-' John goes on.

Amelia glances up from her desk as the screaming from the T.V gets louder, the breaking news story has caught the attention of some of those in the office and they turned the sound up to hear it better.

John the news correspondent was being attacked live on T.V by a woman in a brown business suit, his neck being bitten, was she eating him?

Amelia stood up picking up her phone, her social media account pinging away at her.

The now half bitten necked John was turning for the camera man, a few strands of muscle and ligament dangling on his shoulder, his shirt now crimson with blood as it slipped down his arm, as he stares into the camera he pauses a moment, his eyes blood red, the whites had disappeared, blood dripping from his neck, his sweaty shirt torn to pieces, the picture a blur as the camera is dropped from his grip, the camera catches John grabbing the camera man and doing the same to him as the woman had done to John, it looked like John was eating him. Tearing him apart, scratching at his stomach, biting his neck. The camera man screams trying to get John off him. He then stops and laying still for a moment. John has turned away and glancing round trying to find his next victim, he runs off. The camera man then gets up slowly, he then turns this way and that, also looking for victim, his entrails sagging at his feet.

The picture flicks back to the studio to the shocked presenter, she tries to gather herself together ignoring the tears of

fear falling from her eyes.
Clearing her throat she says;

'I'm not sure what to say… get out of London if you can.'

Amelia looks down at her phone, some of her colleagues at her elbow, watching dumbstruck at the T.V, Amelia opening her social media and is bombarded with videos of these attacks. Not just the individuals attacking others but pregnant women were being attacked most of all. She turns to one of them.

'Look, this was posted in America.'

The video showed of a young woman crying out in pain clutching her belly, then all of a sudden the lower part of her belly bursts with blood and God knows what spilling onto the ground. Horrified by what she was watching Amelia scrolled to a different video, this time a clearly pregnant woman clutched her bump, then the same thing happened, her stomach just… exploded. Something fell from her stomach landing on the floor, just a pool of lumps and blood.

'What the hell is going on?' Whispered the lady standing next to her.

'I don't know, but I think I'm going to go home.' Amelia rushed to her desk gathering her personal belongings, just as she was turning to leave, the Prime Minister appeared on the big T.V.

'Go home. Lock your doors and windows. Do not go outside. This is an emergency broadcast. You must stay indoors.'

At that, Amelia left, she ran to her car turned the engine and locked the doors, when she felt safe to do so she called Jason.

'Hello? Amelia?'

'Jason, you OK?'

'Yeah, have you seen the news?'

'Yes. What is going on?'

'Apparently it is some kind of terror attack.'

'I don't think so Jason, this is happening all over the world. I've seen videos from America, to Russia, from Dubai. This isn't any kind of terrorist attack.'

'Where are you?'

'Just on my way home now, you?'

'Same, meet me there, if you get there before me, pack an over night bag. I think we need to get out of Portsmouth.'

Amelia nodded.

'Amelia? You there?'

Amelia shook her head, 'yes, yes, I'm here, sorry Jason. See you soon, love you.'

'Love you too. Get back safe'.

The call was disconnected. People were running in all directions trying to get back home. Some were pushing others, at one point Amelia had to emergency stop so she didn't hit a young man who was pushed in front of her car. The panic was everywhere, you could feel it in the air. Police were trying to control the violence but with very little effect. She past some shops where people were running out with arms full of food and drink, others being thrown to the ground and the thieves just taking everything they can.

Amelia drove up the driveway, Jason not yet home. She ran through the door and once inside locked it. She ran upstairs and grabbed what she could. She could hear someone trying to get in, she picked up one of her high heeled shoes that she had worn the evening before and crept downstairs ready to strike.

Jason walked through the door and stopped looking up at Amelia, her face full of terror the shoe raised.

'Whoa! It's me, it's me. Do you have a bag packed?'

She nodded and let the shoe fall from her hand. Jason ran up the stairs and hugged her. She felt safe again.

Once they were both packed, changed out of their work clothes and ready to leave, Jason handed Amelia a crow bar, he had a hammer tucked into his belt. Amelia looked at the crow bar in shock.

'Just in case we get attacked, it's spread to Portsmouth, people are being attacked in Southsea.'

Amelia nodded again and they both headed out the front door. Running through the back streets trying to put as much distance as possible between them and what might be coming for them.

'We need to get away from the people. By the looks of things on these video's and news reports, it looks like the more people there are the quicker this spreads.' Jason said.

Amelia made no comment, she couldn't believe what was happening, she kept focused on her breathing, not really paying attention as to where they were going. Next thing she new she was travelling up hill.

'We need to get to the countryside. I reckon a field up between Denmead and Soberton. Somewhere around there. Not very many people, hide in one of the fields until the police, army, whatever can get this under control.' Jason had this all planned out, he probably planned it on his way back from work, picking up the crowbar and hammer. He has seen too many apocalyptic movies.

They reached the top of Portsdown Hill, a helicopter thundered above them, all of a sudden a huge bang and a fireball lit the sky with orange and yellow flame. They had bombed the south part of the city. Amelia clutched at Jason to stay standing, they are already bombing the cities. The government has not got this under control...

Amelia and Jason started to run, run as far away as they could as fast as they could to get away, to stop seeing and hearing the horrors of below. Car's were dumped at the side of the road, jumping between them they finally reach the fields beyond the hill. Distracted by the events going on behind them they didn't realise running to the side of them was a runner, he caught Amelia, dragging her down, pinning her. The pain in her shoulder was immense as the runner bit down hard, pulling at her flesh. Jason grabbed his hammer and smashed it over the runners head cracking the bone. Crying out in fear and anger.

Jason grabbed Amelia and continued running. When Jason let go of Amelia's hand she stood stock still shouting at him to keep running. Jason stopped and looked back at her.

'Amelia, let's go, run!'

'No. You run! Get as far away from me as you can before I change!' Tears streaming down her face. But she didn't feel any different, there was no, change.

They stood in the same spot for sometime waiting. Jason found chains keeping a field secure and threw them to Amelia. She wrapped herself in them, needing Jason's help he bound her arms to her sides and locked the chains. They stopped at a nearby field as darkness crept over them. They slept back to back taking it turns. Amelia continued this way for a few more days but nothing happened. Jason cleaned the wound as best he could using plasters and other material to help the bleeding which did eventually stop.

When Jason was changing the plaster for the second time Amelia asked him where had all the medical kit had come from.

'I've had this bag tucked away for some time. I've always kept a medical kit in it and just stocked up little by little. You never know what shit nature is going to throw at you.'

'It's a good job you have been watching all those end of the world films, I'd be dead if it wasn't for this bag.' Amelia laughed.

Jason shrugged, he liked all those movies, but deep down he knew something was going to happen, he just hoped it wouldn't happen in his life time.

Jason decided to remove the chains on day four as they were walking through more fields.

'I don't know if that is a good idea.'

'Well, you've not changed, watching the videos and news reports people change pretty much as soon as they get bitten and you haven't, it's been four days.'

Amelia sighed and let the chains fall to her feet, she stepped out of them rubbing her arms. On the sixth day they found a small group of people huddled up in a field, none of them asked if they had been bitten, Jason had made sure he hid the bite under Amelia's clothes well so no one could get suspicious, that was were they decided to make the refuge. They scavenged what they could, built fences round a small perimeter and built it up from there, when more and more people begged for refuge they would expand the perimeter to allow for more people to join them. As houses were out of the question tents started to pop up to protect them from the elements, tents for the people and for the vegetable patches. As the years went passed they voted for a council to lead the group of survivors, to decide who is in and if any criminal activity, who was out, they started building with wood and slowly became what they are now. A small community of people just trying to survive.

That was nearly eight years ago and as Amelia and Jason were such a big part within the community they decided if they were to try and have a baby, they would be safe, their baby would be safe, and the people around them would be supportive. How very wrong indeed they were.

◆ ◆ ◆

When Amelia realised she was pregnant she went to her most trusted friend on the council, Eli. She explained that she is immune to the virus and so is the baby, his reaction did not make her feel easy but he soon settled and things went back to normal. As far as he was concerned if she exploded due to her own incompetence that was her problem. He never let go of his weapon all the while he was close to her. As the Autumn turned to winter and winter to spring Amelia's belly grew. The community were polite but started to keep their distance, soon enough Amelia and Jason were avoided altogether.
The council called for a meeting and invited the pair to join them so they could discuss what happens once the baby is born. That was not the discussion that took place.

'How do you know that this baby is not going to kill you?'

'I just know. I told you last week and the week before, all through this pregnancy Eli, this baby does not have the disease.' Amelia sighed, she knew she had to keep her cool. Herself and Jason decided not to tell the council that Amelia had been bitten all those years ago. Their reaction to the baby made the decision for them to keep it quiet, just to be safe.

'How do we know for CERTAIN that this baby isn't going to spark something in you that will make you try and destroy what we have built?'

'You'll need to take her word for it!' Jason was getting agitated and loosing his cool.

'Please Jason, they need to make sure everyone here is safe. Seven years ago women got to around twenty six weeks pregnant and things started to go wrong for them, their babies turned into one of those things, tearing them inside out, I'm 35 weeks and nothing has happened.' Amelia touched her hand to her husbands and they stood in front of the council hand in hand.

'We're sorry Amelia, Jason, but this is not going to work, we cannot risk it. We need to hand you over to the government, we made all the arrangements already. Pack what you need, the truck will be here tomorrow.'

'What? Why have you pulled the government into this?' Amelia felt the fear build inside her.

The government survived, how, no one knows. There is still an attempt to keep the power going as much as possible. As for the Royals, well, they are, as far as everyone is aware, safe and sound. Hidden in their castles.

'IF you are immune and your baby is not carrying the disease they need to know so we can find out how to prevent it in other pregnancies. Get humanity back on its feet, breed again.'

'No, this is not fair, I do NOT consent to this!' Tears of rage building in Amelia's eyes. 'You're just going to hand me over for experimentation? God knows what they will do to me and the baby.'

'We have been here since the beginning, we have helped build this community to how it stands today, to be safe. You cannot be serious on handing us over?' Jason pleaded.

'We've had the community make complaints, they do not feel safe, and with a vote, it was voted that we hand you over. I'm sorry, I truly am.' Eli did look sorry, but Amelia was so angry with him she just glared at him.

'You may leave to collect your things.'
With that, the council left, leaving Amelia in tears and Jason stood dumbfounded at the reaction of the community.

As the sun set Amelia and Jason were packing their over night bags getting ready to leave when they heard footsteps outside. It was Tess and Noah, they heard what the council had decided and made a plan to help Amelia and Jason escape.

'We need to get you out of here.' Whispered Tess her long blonde hair tied up in a ponytail trailing down her back, as soon as Jason let them into their tent.

'We can't just leave, you know how dangerous it is out there, we can't risk Amelia in her condition.' Jason's face was full of panic.

'Jason, we can't let the government have her, God knows what they will do to her and the baby. We have our own bags packed and ready to go outside the perimeter.'

'We did not think the community would be like this, we thought they would have welcomed a baby, especially as being as far gone as you are, that would be enough proof that this baby is no monster. I was certainly looking forward to seeing a baby again, it's been far too long.' Sighed Noah.

Jason looked over to Amelia, her face shinning from the tears. Amelia nodded.

'We can't let them do this to us, Tess is right, it's too dangerous, what if they kill the baby?'

'I know, I know, my main concern is where are we going to go? You can't run or climb walls, or what if the baby decides to come when it isn't ready?'

'It's risky, but it will be worth it when it does come.'

'There is a cabin, in the New Forest, my mum and dad owned it when I was a kid, we stopped going once mum got ill. But I believe it is still there.' Said Noah

'The New Forest? Thats miles away! How do you think we are going to get there? Walk?'

'Precisely. It's a twenty three mile walk, and will take us about 8 hours maybe a bit more. But Jason, Amelia and the baby will be safe there.' Tess tried to smile at Jason to reassure him, but Jason's face was still not convinced.

Amelia grabbed his arm and took him to one side.

'I don't think we have much of a choice Jason. It's going to be a long walk, but we are walking through the country, and there are no cities to try and get through. There will be less runners to avoid, as long as we stay together and avoid the cities we should make it, they are right, it is either go there and have the baby or let the government take us away, were you know you may never see us again.'
Jason sighed touching his wife's face. He bowed his head and with a slight nod whispered; 'OK, let's go.'

The four of them waited until full darkness fell on the camp site. When everyone was in their tent and only the watchers were out guarding the perimeter. With their bags packed with as much food, water, clothes and blankets as they could carry they started one by one to leave the back of the tent.

Tess and Noah went ahead and collected their own bags and they hurried into the night, cutting through fields, keeping away from the houses and other potential sources of life and death.

They walked until they were certain they were a good distance from the camp site with Jason and Noah covering their tracks as the two women walked ahead arm in arm, keeping one eye out for humans and one eye out for any straggling runners.

The sun was starting to rise when Amelia asked if they could stop and rest, her body was starting to ache from the weight of the baby and fatigue from no sleep and a lot of walking.

They found a small ditch that two people could sleep in, using their blankets, they made beds. Amelia and Tess slept first whilst Jason and Noah kept watch sitting on either side of the ditch so they could keep watch at all angles.

All four decided it would be safer to sleep during the day and travel at night, they could see better in the daylight for danger. None of them were prepared for the amount of stops they would have to make for Amelia. Her hips and back were aching and she needed to stop to pee behind a tree or bush, a lot. There were some moments when Amelia felt she had made a huge mistake and wanted to go back to camp and allow for the government to take her away where she would be warm and comfortable, there were other times where she was determined to have this baby on her own terms and attempt to save humanity.

They were on their second night travelling through the country, Noah and Tess were up ahead scouting the area for danger, when Tess noticed a dark shape looming in the distance.
　'Is that a house?'
　'Looks like it, looks abandoned as well.' Noah headed back to Amelia and Jason to let them know what they have found.
　'It could be full of runners.' Jason hesitated.
　'It could be full of food and a warm bed. We need to try and allow for Amelia to sleep in a comfortable bed as much as we can, Tess and I will go ahead and make sure the house is clear before you guys come in.'
　Noah ran back to catch up with Tess as she approached the house, her baseball bat in her hand ready, just in case.
　Amelia and Jason hung back at the entrance gate behind some bushes and waited. The morning was eerily quiet, not a sound of a bird, or the whispering of the trees that surrounded them. The sky started to light up as the moon set and the sun rose which Amelia was grateful for as she needed the rest. Her body was starting to ache terribly and she could feel the baby moving restlessly. It won't be long now till she will be here. After what felt like an age, Noah came round the corner smiling.
　'Come on in.'
Amelia went first with Jason behind her spinning his head from left to right, he could feel the air around him tightening.
　When they stepped through the front door, Tess was busy by the fire pit, she already had some soup in a pot, her long slender arms working to make a fire.
Noah picked up a bundle of blankets, duvets and pillows and laid them down near the fire that was now roaring.

'We found some soup and the water is still running here, the house is clear, looks like the owners left in a hurry. If we keep all the curtains closed and bar the door we should be safe to sleep.' Tess said standing up and stretching.

They all slurped at the soup like they hadn't eaten for days and made themselves as comfortable as possible, all four decided

they would sleep in the front room together. There was one bed upstairs but the stain on the mattress did not appeal to the group, it was safer and cleaner to sleep altogether.

Amelia woke with a start, the sunlight streaming through a gap in the curtains on her face making her hot, she thought she heard something.
She got up and made her way slowly towards the window and twitched the curtain open with shaking fingers to see outside. She was shocked to see someone stood at the gate, his clothes were ripped and he had no shoes on his feet, his eyes the colour of blood and a deep gash in his neck, his blood eyes fixed on the house, she new he could smell them.

'Jason, Noah, Tess, wake up! There are runners outside.' The harsh whisper made Noah jump up and take action immediately. He grabbed his axe, and went over to Jason to shake him awake putting his hammer in his hands.

Tess stirred too grabbing her base ball bat.

'Come away from the window Amelia, grab your stuff me and you will go round the back.' Tess picked up her own things and started to make her way to the kitchen.

Amelia grabbed her bag and her crow bar and followed Tess to the kitchen. There was a smash on the front door with another runner trying to scratch her way in, Jason and Noah ran towards the kitchen and out the back door.

Tess and Jason put their arms around Amelia trying to help

her to run faster Amelia's bump was too heavy, her hips were on fire, she couldn't breathe, she just focused on running not looking behind her.

Noah was shouting something behind them but she couldn't hear what was said, Tess turned around and screamed for Noah, Jason let go of Amelia who kept going heading for a bramble bush in the distance. She dived into it crouching as low as she could, listening so hard all she could hear was the ringing in her ears.

There was rustling in the bush in front of her, raising her crow bar ready to strike whatever was coming towards her. It was Jason followed by Tess, Jason raised his arms

'Whoah, it's me Amelia, it's Jason.' He looked back at Tess tears where streaming down her face.

'Where's Noah?'
Jason looked down, Amelia looked at Tess.

'Where is Noah?' She asked again.

'He... he got caught...' Jason looked at Amelia.

'Let's go before they find us.' Tess crawled through the bush and out the other side followed by the others.

'Tess, I'm so sorry...' Amelia started.

'It's fine... We need to get moving. Put as much distance between us and the runners as possible. Jason do you have the map and compass?'
Jason handed both over.

'It's ok to cry Tess, you just lost your boyfriend.' Said Amelia, putting a hand gently on her shoulder.

Tess shrugged it off. 'We don't have time for that, if we can get you safe, then I will mourn, but until then, we move.' Her face was stern, which caused Amelia to take a step back.
Leaning on a fence Tess looked at the map and the compass and decided they were going in the wrong direction. She turned west and headed out through the fields again.
Amelia and Jason almost running to keep up with her shouted for her to stop.

'We need to know how far we have left to travel Tess. I don't know how much further I can go, this baby is making it very uncomfortable to walk.'

'I think we are close, but I don't know the exact location, only Noah knew exactly where to go and now he is dead. This is your fault, if you had only just let nature do its thing and kill off the human race he would still be here.' Tess turned her back once again and tried to storm off but Amelia caught her arm. She hesitated a moment, she was about to tell Tess that none of them would be here if they let nature run its course, but thought better of it and decided to tell her the truth.

'We decided to have this baby because I'm immune to the virus.'

'How do you know that? You cannot possibly know that!' Amelia pulled down the right side of her t-shirt to show Tess her shoulder. There was a shiny red round mark with small indents that looked like human teeth marks.
Tess took a step back.

'When did this happen?'

'When it first started, I was bitten by one, I got caught and he bit me on the shoulder, there was a lot of blood, I swung my crow bar at him but he would not let go, Jason killed him with his hammer, and then nothing. I waited, I put chains around myself, Jason was not allowed near me, but nothing happened. After a few days I realised that I must be immune, that this virus cannot kill me, that's when I knew that I can carry children. Jason and I tried for years and this time we got lucky. We knew then that the world was ready for the human race again and we can start over again and maybe stop being greedy and look after this planet and nature might not hit back so hard this time.'

'Shit Amelia who else knows?'

'No one, just us three. I couldn't exactly shout about it or I would have been carted straight off, just like what they are trying to do to me now.'

The three of them walked calmly, Tess slowed down and linked her arm through Amelia's to help with her walking as she talked, she was getting breathless. They started to see more deserted buildings, broken windows, and cracks in the roads where the weeds were trying to poke their heads up.

'This could start to get dangerous, keep your weapons up and wits about you, I think we are starting to approach the edge of Southampton.' Jason whispered.

'Could we not go around? It looks like we managed to escape Hedge End and I think we should have walked through that.' Using a tree Tess got the map out again and marked where they were.

'It looks like if we carry on the B3354 we can avoid a lot of the villages and walk through the fields again. The trouble is it does look like we are going to need to go through either a village or try and get through some of Southampton.'

'That is far too dangerous, you know that Tess, we cannot risk it.'

'Well, Jason, we are going to have to there is no other way, if it was that much of a problem you should have mentioned this before we left the camp in Denmead.'

'Well that was not on my mind, you said it would be safe, this is not safe!'

'Shut up, the pair of you, I've been bitten before, I'm sure it won't be a problem again, just make sure you run or fight with everything you have. It won't be long now before the baby arrives anyway, I have a feeling it's coming within the next couple of days whether we have reached our destination or not. Now let's move it!'

Amelia paced ahead with crow bar at the ready just in case any runners did stray too close to her. They were lucky, they managed to get through to Southampton Airport and skipped through the country heading west.

Just as they had reached the town of Rushington Amelia started getting pains in her side, she grabbed Jason's arm;

'I think the contractions are starting.'

'Oh God, not now... we're not there yet!'

'I think we're ok for now as my waters haven't broken but we are certainly not far off.' Amelia tried to reassure Jason so he wouldn't panic but it was too late and panic started setting in already.

He quickened his pace almost dragging Amelia with him to catch up with Tess and let her know what is going on.

After camping out for a few hours in a derelict house they finally reached the edge of the forest. It had taken them a total of four days to get there as Amelia needed to stop and rest for a long time before having the energy to start walking again.

As they walked deeper into the forest Amelia's pain was getting stronger, as the sun set she was almost giving up hope that they will find the cabin that Noah had told them about when Tess shouted out. There looming in the distance was a wooden roof surrounded by trees and bushes. It looked perfect.

Jason stopped suddenly.

The world around them became very quiet. No bird song, no wind stirring up the bushes, no sound of any kind.

Tess came running towards Amelia, she sprinted past raising her weapon as she did, the sound of a bat colliding with bone struck the air. Amelia turned round just in time to see Tess trying to fight off seven runners, Jason immediately raised his weapon running towards them.

All Amelia could think about was getting to that cabin she ran ahead clutching the bottom of her bump running through the pain. She felt like she was wetting herself as she was running and realised her waters were breaking with every step she took.

She burst through the door, weapon raised and cried out in pain, doubling over, her luck was still with her as the cabin was empty.

She crawled over to the fire and laid on the old mould covered rug that was left, removing her underwear she had to start pushing, every instinct in her told her to push.

There was a noise at the door, Tess had come running back to be with her, she was covered in blood, whether that be her own or the runners she did not know, Tess was barricading the door with all the furniture she could find.

'Where's Jason?' Amelia managed to puff out.

Tess did not answer but told her to keep pushing, the babies head

was in view.
Finally, the baby girl was out screaming, scrunching her tiny fists her eyes closed. Tess wrapped her in one of the towels they had carried with them and handed her over to an exhausted Amelia.

'Tess, where is my husband?'

'Im so sorry. He... he got bit they swarmed him and...' Tess could say no more tears running down her face.

◆ ◆ ◆

It had been ten years since Amelia gave birth to her daughter, the day her husband became one of them. She saw him occasionally, wondering through the tall grass, through the bushes looking, hunting for them. He never found them.

At seven years old Jane was already well skilled with combat. She could effortlessly and soundlessly creep through the tall grass and had already made her first kill of a runner. She was fearless.

Jane continued to grow up unknowing of what the world was like before the virus hit, all she knew was her mother and Tess were scared of the world beyond their cabin. She often tried to convince them of leaving, going back to their original camp to show them and see that a cure is out there, but Amelia would have none of it. She tried to explain why they couldn't leave, that the government would have all of them, test them until they died to see if they can cure the world. Jane did not understand what her mothers problem was, that if she was the one to hold the cure than surely she should be shared.

Tess was often the one that would dwindle the arguments down, stand between them and remind them of what happens if you get caught by a runner, but this did not put Jane off. She would often sneak out, as she got older, she began to go further.

It was when Jane turned eighteen, that was when she decided to leave the cabin for good. The night before she cooked a good meal and made sure Amelia and Tess had a lovely night, so that they could remember their last time together for a while, to make sure the memory of Jane was a good one.

She left just before dawn, carrying with her some food and water that she had been stocking up on and keeping hidden for a while. She was equipped with her dads hammer, her own trusty rounders bat both tucked into her belt at each side. Jane travelled as far as she could as quickly as she could, not even knowing if she was going in the right direction. Her mother would not show her fellow campmates that the human race can survive this, but she sure will, if they are still there. Its been eighteen years since Amelia, Jason, Tess and Noah left the camp. Who knows what was left of it now but Jane was determined to find out.

DENISE LESLEY

Coming soon....

The Little Book of Quests

About the Author

Denise Lesley grew up in Portsmouth, England, where she lives now with her boyfriend and beloved dog Cooper.
She attends The Open University studying for a BA Hons degree English Literature and Creative Writing. Lesley plans on graduating in the spring of 2022.

Lesley started writing stories from a young age, her inspiration for writing are authors such as Charles Dickens, J.R.R Tolkien and J.K Rowling. She hopes that one day her stories will inspire other young writers to tell theirs.

Printed in Great Britain
by Amazon